Say "whit like" to Rara Roggy, Orkney's peediest heroine. Then join her on a magical journey of discovery as she attempts to outwit the wicked Witchypoo and defend her strange new friends from the gigantic killer spider!

An enchanting children's tale of a peedie girl with a BIG heart.

Rara's Peedie Adventure

Michelle G. Robertson

Publishing by

Rara Roggy Publishing

ISBN No. 978-1-902957-33-3

Contents

For Liam, Dale, Roselle, Ramsay, Zara and Max

Introduction

This is a story for all those who believe in magic. For the non-believers, here is a warning: Beware of smelly old ladies who own vicious black cats and even more importantly, be very careful what you wish for. It just might come true!

Have you ever noticed that the most honest people on the planet are young children? As we get older, we learn to tell lies. Sometimes they are only peedie white lies like, "oh no Aunty Fiona, of course your bum doesn't look big in that dress." Sometimes they are whoppers like, "no I didn't break that, it was like that when I got here!"

Young children are brilliant at saying exactly what is on their mind without telling fibs. They are amazing in many other ways too. Like little sponges, they soak up every piece of information which surrounds them. They constantly ask the question WHY?

"Why are baboons bottoms red?"

"Why do beans give us windy botties?"

"Why are feet smelly?"

Rara Roggy was one such remarkable little child.

Rara Roggy

Rara Roggy lived on the beautiful, magical island of Orkney. She was an incredibly inquisitive child who questioned everything. She wanted to know why things existed and how they worked. Rara knew very little about witches but that was about to change!

Witches despise inquisitive children, they think of them as being extremely naughty. Would you like to know what witches do to children they consider naughty? Then please read on.

Rara Roggy wished that she was BIG because big people, (especially grown-ups) get to make up the rules and do all the cool things. Whilst the peedie, younger ones HAVE to follow the rules, b-o-r-i-n-g!

Rara's parents explained to her, that by eating her dinners (including green vegetables) she WOULD grow big and her dream of being able to do all the things she wanted to, would come true. Unfortunately Rara didn't believe them and continually refused to eat properly.

"Come on Rara" her mother would beg "eat your greens."

"Why?" She'd reply.

"Because they're good for you. Try some sprouts."

"Urgh, they smell like bottom burps"

"Spinach then"

"Nope, that's like seaweed"

"Dear oh dear Rara, what will we do with you? Can you please eat your meat, it's a rump steak. It will make you big and strong."

"A rump steak? Ewwwww, why oh why would I eat a cow's bottom!"

"Honestly Rara, one of these days you'll regret not eating your dinners and then it'll be too late!"

charming!

Rara Roggy's family and friends

Ro

Rara longed to be marvellously clever just like her big sister Ro.

Ro had a very special ability. She knew things were going to happen before they actually did. For example, she could tell you that the phone was about to ring and then seconds later....... brrring brrring, sure enough, it would. She knew what the weather would be like each day. She even knew all of the answers in her exams at school. Rara thought her big sister was wonderful.

Dae and Rammy

Rara also adored her two older brothers Dae and Rammy. They were twins bursting with energy and vitality. Both of them exceptional gymnasts. They were so fast and bendy that people often thought that the boys' bones were made from rubber!

They actually thought of themselves as superheroes and sometimes got into terrible predicaments. The rest of the family referred to the boys as "double trouble". They were daredevils. Always ready for the next adventure, the more dangerous the better!

Leo

The one thing Rara wished for most of all was to be VERY big and VERY strong just like her eldest brother Leo. He was sixteen. Dae and Rammy were always marvelling at the width of his biceps or clapping and cheering with delight at how many one arm push –ups he could do.

He could bend metal bars as if they were made from liquorice.

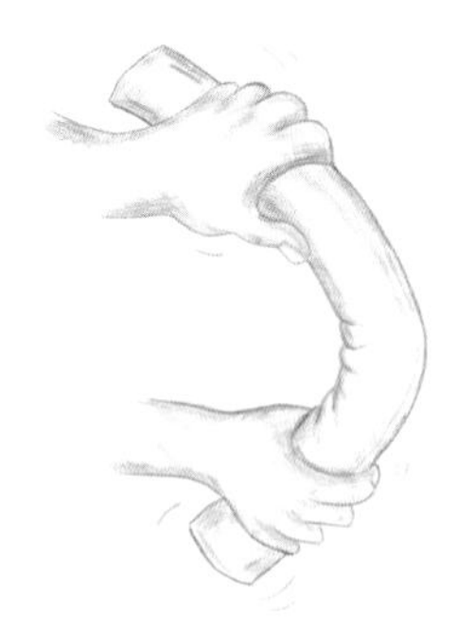

On many occasions he attempted without success to persuade Rara to eat broccoli: "It's a SUPER food which contains iron". He'd say. Leo explained to her that the green vegetables had

given him his super strength, allowing him to pull trees out of the ground by the time he was Rara's age.

"BUT, I DON'T EAT GREENS!" she'd shout.

Father

Rara's father was a busy and somewhat eccentric business man. He worked all around the Globe. His first evening back home after a long journey would be spent with the children listening, captivated by his spellbinding tales of exotic faraway lands. His stories of unusual people and fantastical

creatures kept the children totally enthralled and filled their sleep with the most exciting dreams.

Mother

Rara's dear mother was always on the move, constantly attending to dishes, clothes, dogs, washing, ironing and cooking. Her great love, other than her children, was painting and her studio was filled with many wonderful pictures.

Rara would often ask her mother "Why don't I have SPECIAL powers like the others?" Her mother's reply was always the same.

"Darling Rara, the others have no more SPECIAL powers than you or I. You just have to BELIEVE in yourself."

But Rara did BELIEVE in many things: fairies, goblins, imps and most of all witches. Her fertile imagination was fuelled by her Grandparents tales of talking animals, exploding goblins and huge blue hairy snow beasts! Rara's parents assured her that these 'things' were merely 'make believe.' But Rara knew different, she had learned a great deal about witches first hand.

Witchypoo

The trickiest and nastiest person in Rara's life was Wilhemia Boon, better known to all as Witchypoo.

Witchypoo was a horrid old lady who disliked inquisitive children and had a very special way of punishing them.

She was as ancient as Skara Brae and as mystical as Maes Howe.

Her only friend in the world was Rara's mother and that was simply because Rara's mother could find good in everyone, no matter how well hidden it was!

Witchypoo's hair was as black as the midnight sky. Her pale face was shaped like a half moon. Her chin and nose had huge hairy warts, which wobbled as she spoke. Her rotten teeth resembled the Standing Stones, the woman was truly frightening.

Witchypoo had a peedie body and a twisted humpy back which was as bent as a butchers bacon hook. Her long bony arms stuck out from her black shapeless dress, a garment she wore every single day without exception. It was extremely smelly.

Witchypoo lived in a peedie cottage. Its chimney puffed the most disgusting green, pungent smoke. Rara often wondered if the smoke came from a cauldron within,

bubbling over with eyes of newts and bats blood!

Children who walked past would scurry along as quickly as they could, holding their breath and nipping their noses to stop themselves catching witchypooitis!

Witchypoo's only companion was a mangy old black cat.

The cat

The cat was the scruffiest, smelliest creature you could ever meet. It looked as though it had been run over by a truck, thrown against a wall, dropped down a well then blown up by dynamite! Cute and cuddly it was most certainly not! Anyone seeing the cat at first glance would genuinely feel pity, but appearances can be deceptive, because despite the cat appearing peedie and forlorn. It was in fact a mad bad cat.

So mean was the cat that whenever Rara and her sister Ro walked past with their dogs, Kona and Belle, the wicked cat would stalk them, chasing them down the street with their tails between their legs!

How could such a pitiful looking cat be so brave and spread abject fear into every dog in the area? Could it be Witchcraft perhaps? Was the mouldy moggy really a witch's cat? Rara Roggy was about to find out just how Witchy, Witchypoo really was!

The lunchtime problem

It was lunchtime and just like every other lunchtime on every other day Rara was far too busy playing to sit still and eat her meal. Rara's mother simply did not understand how busy Rara actually was. The sun was shining and Rara wanted to be outside, soaking up some rays and playing with her toys.

"Rara, please sit in your chair, your food is getting cold" begged her mother. Everyone else in the family had sat down ages ago and were half way through their meal. Rara glared at everyone then reluctantly threw herself into her chair.

"Okay", she thought, "I'll do it, but I won't enjoy

it, and it better be over quickly". Meal times were boring, Rara dreaded them because:

Number One: They interrupted valuable play time.

Number Two: They ALWAYS involved green vegetables, YUK! Rara wouldn't even eat green sweets nowadays!

Number Three:
Finally and most annoyingly, during meal times someone would ALWAYS utter the same awful sentence. "If you don't eat you'll always be peedie"

Mother put the plate of food down in front of Rara. As usual, there was green stuff on it. "Agghhh"!

Now there was only one thing in the whole world that could make meal times an even

worse torture than normal and that was having Witchypoo in the house. She would occasionally get invited by mother, Heaven knows why? Rara did not believe nor care about the "she's got no one else" theory which her mother claimed to be true. It was awful having the wrinkly old fusspot present. Rara resented it. The ancient old crone arrived at least once a week for food or sometimes just for afternoon tea. Either way it was wretched.

Mother always felt compelled to help people in need and she regarded Witchypoo as a needy case worthy of kindness and attention. Rara on the other hand was of the opinion that the only thing Witchypoo was in need of was a good hot bath, plenty of deodorizer and a trip to the chemist for as much wart remover and vanishing cream as she was able to carry!

There were many reasons for Rara not enjoying the horrid old bag's company. Here are a few:

Number One: The PUNGENT smell. No one knew exactly what it was or even where it was coming from, but to try and give a proper understanding then imagine this; a pile of filthy smelly old socks with dirty rats living inside them. Some of the rats are dead and their bodies are decaying. The few rats which are still alive are rotting and rancid. They are eating that awful smelly blue veiny cheese, which is so incredibly old, that mushrooms and mould are growing on it! That's how smelly Witchypoo could be on a good day! Can you imagine the stench in the height of summer? It was enough to frighten grown men!

Number Two:
Even more dangerous than the odour was the worry that someone might actually see the Witch enter the house and then Rara's street credibility would be right out of the window! Oh the shame of it, the terrible news would spread

like wildfire. The next thing you know all of the kids would be chanting "Rara has Witchypoo-itis!" Rara made the family promise not to tell any of her school mates about Witchypoo's visits.

Number Three: Rara despised conversing with Witchypoo. The rotten Wrinkly was so opinionated. You could guarantee hearing the dreaded sentence from the miserable old crone "If ye dinna eat yer dinner ye'll nae get big, ye'll stay peedie forever."

Number Four: Rara would inevitably get a row for telling the truth! How unfair is that? Simple questions like, "why do you smell like sick?" would get Rara into a whole lot of trouble. Rara felt that Witchypoo's visits were utterly tiresome.

Rara's brothers and sister on the other hand thought it was hilarious having Witchypoo in the house. Even Ro put up with it despite her deductive powers not working when Witchypoo was around. This particular day was no exception. The fun began shortly after Witchypoo arrived and sat at the table.

“Uuuurgh” whispered Dae as he sat at the table screwing up his face and covering his mouth, “look at those hairy warts hanging off her face. They’re putting me off my food.”

(They did seem to have a life of their own. They actually appeared to move at will. It was quite unnerving.)

Rammy began to giggle “why do you think mother invites her?”

“Probably ‘cos mother’s scared Witchypoo will cast a spell on her otherwise!” replied Dae speaking out of the corner of his mouth. This made Rammy laugh so much some food fell out of his mouth and back on to his plate.

“Holy guacaMOLE” giggled Dae as he gripped his sides for fear they might split. He then casually slipped a joke green sweetie on to

Witchyppo's plate, (you know, the type that turns the unsuspecting victims tongue bright green.) He put it right beneath the peas where she wouldn't see it. Rammy began laughing uncontrollably and the dinner table shook.

"That's not very nice" pointed out Ro. "She's an old lady you know." She then lowered her voice and whispered through gritted teeth "now stop making fun of her warts and eat your food!" Ro looked at the boys in turn with her most disapproving glare.

The meal continued in relative silence. Only the adults converesed and gratefully nodded towards mother as their food was happily consumed.

Suddenly Leo chuckled to himself and almost choked. He cleared his throat, then leaned over the table and whispered to the other children "I know why mother invites her! It's because she's about 150 years old and when she falls off her perch, she'll leave all her money to us!" He slapped the table and winked. Then all the boys burst out laughing, including Father! Mother elbowed a still giggling Father fiercely in the

ribs. At this juncture his face was bright red! Mother then reminded everyone to behave, gave them the 'evil eye' and hurriedly cleared the dishes.

Witchypoo wiped her face with a napkin then smiled and graciously thanked mother for the delicious meal. As she smiled her rancid green tongue wriggled like a snake behind her rotten teeth, which were now almost glowing with the same awful colour. Dae and Rammy dashed from the table and ran from the room. Howls of laughter erupted in the hallway as they fell to the floor in hysterics.

Rara at this point had eaten next to nothing. She was just about to leave the table along with the

rest of the children when Witchypoo coughed and cackled. "Ahem, not eating yer dinner then?" She smiled her wicked wonky, wiley, witchy smile. Rara nonchalantly shook her head and began to climb from the table.

All of a sudden Rara began to get an odd cold feeling. It ran all the way down into her tummy and through her back. She glanced back at the table and there was Witchypoo, glaring down at her with her long wart riddled nose twitching away like a mouldy pepperami. "Ye must want to be peedie then" she snipped again and with that, the smelly old flea bag pressed her wizened, wrinkly finger on Rara's forehead. A sharp cold feeling struck Rara through her head and down her neck. It was so powerful that she stumbled backwards. Slightly dazed but utterly unrepentant and undaunted, Rara thrust out her chest and faced Witchypoo.

"Yes, I DO WISH TO BE PEEDIE ACTUALLY!" She declared and rapidly skipped out of the room rubbing her now throbbing head.

Rara hadn't noticed the way Witchypoo cackled quietly to herself after touching Rara's forehead. It was in a most unusual and sinister way.

Perhaps if Rara had picked up on this, she would have been somewhat unnerved and slightly more prepared for what was about to happen next . . .

The peedie adventure

Rara bounced outside to the back garden with all her toys tumbling onto the grass beside her.

What a glorious day, much too nice to be stuck in the house eating vegetables Rara thought. The garden was bursting full of beautiful brightly coloured flowers. Sweet scents and buzzing insects filled the air.

Rara lay on the grass completely motionless and stared up at the lovely wispy clouds. They were disappearing, almost melting into the bright blue sky as if someone were stirring them with a spoon. Blissfully she closed her eyes.

This was perfect, being outside in the sun without any nagging parents or annoying neighbours.

Rara wished she lived in the garden instead of the house. It was so peaceful and calm.

Summer days in Orkney are outstandingly beautiful, the sky appears to go on forever and the grass seems more lush and green than anywhere else in the world. Rara felt as though she was in Heaven.

Rara thought about Witchypoo's parting gesture and decided that she didn't want to grow big, peedie was just fine. She rubbed her head again. It was throbbing slightly, on the spot where Witchypoo had touched her. Rara closed her eyes thoughtfully and drifted slowly into a hazy daydream.

When Rara opened her eyes again she noticed that things were totally different, startlingly different. The sky appeared to be a million miles away and she was lying in this strange giant forest with great trees pointing to the sky. Was this still Rara's garden?

Rara rubbed her eyes and blinked. This was a very strange place. She shook her head, closed her eyes once more and opened them again. She'd hoped that everything would have returned to normal but alas, it had not. Feeling very unsure and uneasy but knowing that she couldn't just stand there all day gawping, Rara began to walk a little way amongst the incredibly tall trees.

That was when she saw a huge plastic figure. It was lying on its side between the trees. It had long blonde curly hair. It appeared to be a giant sized doll, just like the 'swimming beach' Barbie

she had been lying next to on the grass only moments earlier. Had it grown or had Rara shrunk?

Then suddenly, without any warning the most frightening sound echoed through the trees. It was like an earthquake, rumbling and crashing noises filled the air. The trees and the soil trembled. Rara fell to the ground. Her heart was racing and so was her mind but nothing could prepare her for what she was about to see.

A giant faceless serpent rose up into the air. It thrashed from side to side throwing dirt and stones everywhere. Then the ground beneath Rara erupted!

Unbridled fear filled Rara's chest then travelled to her throat, burning all the way. Horror and panic struck. The giant serpent spat out a foul smelling slime onto Rara's face. She stumbled and fell to her knees, head in hands, scared senseless.

At first Rara thought it might be a dinosaur because of its size, but it had no legs, nor a head! It continued swaying as if smelling the air. It looked like a giant earth worm! It was the most horrid thing she had ever seen. As it rose higher Rara felt sure that it was trying to sniff her out. She curled up into a tiny ball and tried to be invisible.

Suddenly the creature brought its huge throbbing body down right next to Rara. She kept her eyes tightly shut and held her breath. In the darkness of her mind she prayed for it to go away. The worm heaved itself further out of the ground and touched the Barbie doll, rocking it gently. Rara prayed that it wouldn't come closer and squash her, or worse still, eat her!

After what seemed like an eternity of poking and stroking the doll with its purple body, the worm suddenly stopped moving.

What was it doing Rara thought to herself, did it know that she was there? Was it waiting for her to make one tiny movement then it would attack her? She had to get rid of it before it got her.

Rara jumped up. She ran as fast as her legs could carry her and dived behind the doll. She remembered that on its back was a button which made the dolls arms paddle up and down in a swimming motion. With all of her might she pushed the button and the dolls arms swung into action. They came chopping down on top of the giant worm, smacking it with full

force. WHACK! It rapidly slid back underground, leaving nothing but a shell shocked Rara and a silvery trail. "That was disgusting" gasped Rara.

After composing herself and cleaning the soil from her clothes, Rara thought she must be dreaming and everything would be fine the moment she awoke.

Just then, another rumbling sound reached Rara's ears but this time it was accompanied by a hollow ache in her tummy. "Ooh" she grumbled, "I wish I'd eaten my lunch, I'm ever so hungry now. I could eat anything".

"And so could I!" quipped another voice from behind the trees.

The thing with eight legs

"Who on Earth said that?" whispered Rara, her eyes desperately scanning the area. She didn't recognize the voice, it sounded female, yet weird and raspy.

Inquisitively Rara edged through the trees and

eventually came upon an opening. This area looked just like the rockery in her back garden, only much, much bigger! There, before her stood the lovely Primula Scotica which Rara had planted only a few weeks earlier. Rara surveyed the area carefully. This WAS the back garden! Rara recognized the garden gnome with his breeks pulled down smiling cheekily back at her. Rara had shrunk!

It was then that Rara noticed something completely unfamiliar. It was the owner of the

terrible voice. On a huge rock, sat the biggest, hairiest spider Rara had ever seen. It was colossal. The spider had so many eyes Rara didn't have a clue which one to look at!

"What exactly are you?" questioned the spider tilting its head slightly. It looked Rara up and down quite disapprovingly. Fluttering its extremely long eyelashes it proceeded to caress itself with its fat hairy brown legs.

"I'm a girl, a human p-person" stammered Rara.

Ordinarily the only spiders which Rara was able to tolerate were the tiny money spiders which often appeared in the greenhouse. Anything larger would have Rara screaming and running for the fly bat!

"Are you a spider?" croaked Rara, whose mouth was so terribly dry with fear that her teeth were sticking to her lips.

"Oh, I'm much more than JUST a spider, little girl. I'm the top of the food chain around here. You get the picture, don't you Pipsqueak?" Rara became immobile. Her whole body was frozen to the spot. "You can stop grinning at me right now Girly" hissed the spider spitting all over Rara in the process. Rara tried her hardest to lick her lips and compose her face. She certainly didn't want to anger the spider any further!

Just then a rustling, buzzing noise emerged from behind Rara's head. Cautiously she glanced around. To her absolute horror she saw a terrified bee all tangled up and struggling for its life in the huge spider's web. Rara could hear the bee's pitiful cries. They sounded simply awful, just like a baby. "The poor thing" she whispered to herself and managed to accidentally bite her bottom lip so hard that it began to bleed. The Spider immediately noticed the blood on Rara's lip and leaned closer. Saliva dribbled from its huge mouth. Rara felt its hot foul-smelling breath blowing through her hair. Once more, fear gripped her.

"Staying for lunch?" questioned the spider as it leaned closer and hungrily ran its black beady

eyes over Rara. A shiver ran through Rara's body like an icy wind. It was so shocking that it made her shake uncontrollably from head to toe. "It looks like a two course meal today" slurped the spider as it licked the saliva from its lips. Rara shuffled backwards to ensure she was out of the spider's reach.

Rara told herself to be brave, "Good stuff comes in peedie bundles" she whispered beneath her breath. That's what Little Grandma had always taught her. Then she gulped and quietly cleared her throat. She knew that she had to think on her feet or she would end up inside that horrid spider! Boldly Rara looked straight at the spider and spoke in a loud, clear voice. "You're a very beautiful spider, aren't you?" (Rara had never told such a whopping lie in her entire life, but

she hoped this one might just save her from being eaten!)

"Yes, how very observant of you little girl, I am THE most beautiful spider in the world and have hundreds of suitors. Every male spider in the garden wants to marry me but generally I just eat them." The spider smiled regally and fluttered its eyelashes quite pleased with its wretched self.

The poor bee's cries grew louder and stronger. They began echoing through the air, screeching like nails on a blackboard. "Erm, Miss Spider, what's that bee doing up there?" questioned Rara breathlessly. Her heart was racing but she tried to give the appearance of absolute calm. The spider glanced at the bee and laughed mockingly

"Oh him, well he was here FIRST you see, so he's going to be the FIRST course. He's really just been hanging around waiting for the SECOND course to arrive and here YOU are!"

Now this was definitely not a good development. The day had gone from bad to

much, MUCH worse. What Rara needed was a cunning plan and she needed it fast!

The great escape

Rara's trembling little hands were shaking in her dungaree pockets. She was frantically wracking her brain for a plan when WHAM, a brilliant idea emerged! The tips of Rara's fingers had inadvertently stumbled upon an old packet of bubble gum.

"W-wait a minute Miss spider" Rara stammered as she held her hand out towards the monster. "Why have only two courses? A spider as special as you surely deserves three." She opened the packet and showed the pieces of bubble gum to the spider. Rara watched, waited and crossed the fingers on the hand still behind her back,

hoping to goodness that the nasty spider would be stupid enough to fall for her trick. The spider greedily eyed the bubble gum. Rara realized that the spider was considering her proposal. Then quick as a flash the fiendish spider pounced and snatched every piece of bubble gum from Rara's hand. Rara watched in absolute amazement as the spider opened its mouth and popped in the lot, paper and all!

The spider began slowly chewing, murmuring away to itself. It rolled its eyes round and round then stroked itself as if in a trance.

What it didn't realize was that every time it opened its jaws a tiny sliver of long stretchy gum was attaching to the corners of its huge mouth. Then with each stroke of its legs the gum was pulled across its body, clinging to every long brown hair that it touched. The spider was in ecstasy, enjoying every single second of gum chewing pleasure.

Before long, and without the spider even realizing it, more than half of the hideous creature was covered in bright pink, stretchy, strawberry flavoured gooey bubble gum.

This was Rara's only chance to escape. She dodged past the spider and nimbly climbed a nearby flower. The spider saw Rara dart past and tried to follow but only succeeded in becoming even more tangled in the gum. It couldn't even speak let alone move! "Yep" laughed Rara, "you're a bully alright and you know what else? The bigger they are the harder they fall!" Rara's Poppa used to say that about the big fat goblins who inhabited his garden and he was right. Just because someone or something is bigger than you it doesn't mean you have to be afraid of them!

Once Rara reached the top of the flower she began feeling very brave indeed. If a peedie girl the size of a bug could outwit and defeat a monstrous giant spider, then she was capable of anything!

As Rara carefully surveyed the area, her eyes fell upon the vegetable patch. There were dozens of neat rows of peas, rocket, courgettes, potatoes plus hundreds of beautiful plump raspberries. Her aching stomach rumbled as her legs carried her nose closer and closer to the fresh smelling food. Rara's mouth watered as she peered through the plastic mesh at the sweet juicy raspberries.

"Ladies first!" shrieked an excitable ladybird. It bustled forward and barged Rara sideways into a rather crusty looking woodlouse.

"Do you mind!" complained the twitchy woodlouse, in a rickety dry voice.

"Oh I do beg your pardon" replied Rara "But I'm not pushing in. I don't wish to eat any of this stuff. Why would I? It's awful. Why would anyone in fact?" The ladybird and woodlouse glared at Rara in total disbelief.

"Then why are you here? Why do you have a slobbery mouth and why do you have a rumbly tum?" asked the ladybird, crossing its arms and narrowing its eyes into tiny slits. Rara began to ask herself the same question. Why was she here? Why was the food (which she would normally detest) making her feel so hungry?

"Why?" said Rara thoughtfully as she scratched her head and rubbed her chin.

"Why, why, why!" grumbled the woodlouse. "Is that all you can say? How about doing something useful, like getting us through

this mesh, we're starving! She's got a broken wing and can't fly" He pointed to the now utterly embarrassed ladybird. "That's not all. I need moisture. I have gills and need to keep damp otherwise I can't breathe!" With that the woodlouse coughed and fell on to its back "If that big old spider finds us, we're supper!" he shouted, kicking and spluttering all over the place.

Rara gazed upon the two pitiful and distressed creatures. "Don't worry about the spider" she reassured them. "I've already fixed her and I know just how to help you."

Rara quickly walked around the mesh cage, inspecting it all very carefully. There was no way any of them could get through. The holes were too small.

Then Rara remembered. Each corner of the cage was tied with string. She could untie it, grab some food for them all and then make it secure to keep it safe from all the other insects. "Okay folks" said Rara cheerily, "you stay here and I'll be back before you can say arachnophobia." The two creatures looked at each other

doubtfully as Rara scaled the mesh cage toward the string ties. After several minutes Rara re-appeared, pockets bulging with rocket, peas and raspberries. She jumped down next to the failing woodlouse and began squeezing a huge raspberry into his open mouth. Almost immediately he sat up and what could have been a grin appeared on his scaly face.

"Thank you clever little one," he said gratefully. "I thought I was a gonner." The ladybird shuffled towards Rara and cuddled her tightly.

"Thank you, you're a Hero" she said blushing redder than ever.

They sat for a moment and smiled at one another, quite happily enjoying each other's company, as friends often do. Rara passed some of the food to the ladybird, who nodded and murmured a little "thank you", before guzzling down peas and raspberries as if her life depended on it.

Before long, most of the food had been consumed. Without even realising it, Rara had munched through two whole pea pods, three giant raspberries and a piece of rocket which was as long as her arm. "Delicious." She said and was just about to eat some more when the terrified cries of the tangled bee echoed through the vegetable patch.

Reluctantly Rara threw down the remaining food. Her tummy was still half empty, but she knew that she must rescue the trapped bee. She said a quick farewell to the ladybird and the woodlouse and headed off towards the bee.

Rara was beginning to feel a little bit like an invincible superhero. Strong and brave just like her brothers. "Hang in there Buddy. I'm going to help you," she promised the bee. Then pulled

out the broken ruler which she always carried in the front pocket of her dungarees.

Tricks and tools of the trade

This simple plastic ruler was an amazing tool. It started life as an ordinary shatterproof ruler from Bruce's Stores. However, just like every other boy or girl of a certain age, Rara had found the temptation too great to find out whether the ruler WAS actually shatterproof. So one day she sat at her desk and bent the ruler as far as it would go and SNAP! It broke magnificently well. It was now the shape of a jagged dagger. Rara had showed it to her brothers, they thought it was absolutely brilliant, so from that moment onwards Rara kept the ruler with her at all times.

The ruler had over the last few months proved to be an invaluable tool on many separate occasions. This was to be its greatest moment yet.

Where would I BEE without you

Using the ruler like a knife, Rara sliced at the web entangling the poor bee. The silk was so incredibly strong that Rara had to saw with all her might.

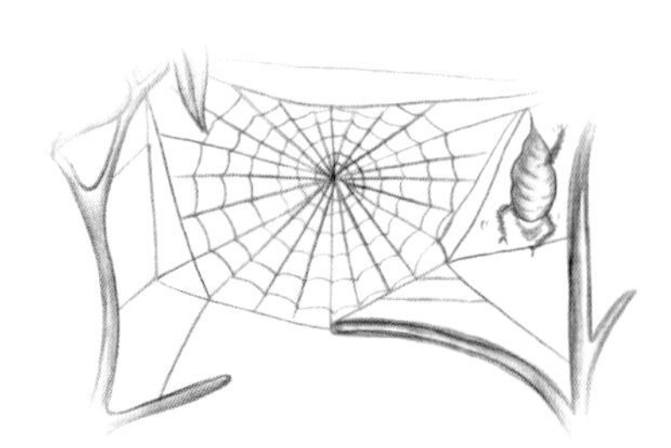

Beads of sweat appeared on her forehead and began dripping down her dirty cheeks. After what seemed like an age Rara finally made it through the web and parts of the bee's body began emerging.

It was becoming clear to Rara that the bee was extremely large and also somewhat scary looking, but Rara bravely gulped away the fear and thought about what Granny often said. "Friends come in all shapes and sizes." Rara immediately decided that any victim of the

dreaded spider must surely be a friend to Rara.

Slowly but surely she freed the frightened creature and slid the ruler back into her pocket, it was a marvellous secret weapon.

The bee was black and yellow and quite furry to the touch. He possessed the most amazing huge eyes, five of them in fact! Rara stepped back and allowed the bee to straighten himself out. It must have been most uncomfortable being trapped in the spider's web Rara thought.

"Where is the spider?" questioned the newly freed bee. "Don't worry about her" laughed Rara, "she won't be bothering you again, like all bullies she came to a sticky end." The grateful bee then placed its front legs on Rara's shoulders and gently kissed her on the cheek. "Oh, I've never been kissed by a bee before."

Rara giggled and for some strange reason her cheeks flushed bright pink. The bee stood up straight to his full height and looked Rara right in the eye "My name is Max and I am forever in your debt. Thank you for saving my life." His delicate buzzing tones rang sweetly in Rara's ears.

"Hey, no problem Max, it was my pleasure, you're my bee buddy!" The bee bowed its head and then slowly rose up and spoke very softly

"Is there anything I can do to repay you? If it is within my power, then it is yours." Rara smiled at Max, he was simply lovely.

All of a sudden Rara's emotions got the better of her. She began to feel very sad indeed. Not only was she still extremely hungry, but she realized for the first time that it was actually getting late. She really wanted to go back home and see her family but the house was too far away, it would take her forever. Rara was too peedie to walk all that way back before nightfall.

Everyone would be worried sick about her. She imagined her dear Mother crying inconsolably.

A frantic Father would be trying to calm things down. Everyone ill with worry, it was simply terrible.

Rara put her head in her hands and began to weep. Long wet streaks ran down her dirt smeared cheeks. Unsightly red blotches began to appear on her face and neck from crying so hard.

Max could stand it no longer. He gently cradled Rara in four of his legs then hovered up into the air. "I shall take you home Rara, back to your family and I shall never forget what you did for me. Please don't cry anymore."

The unusual pair rose into the sky soaring above the flowers, then over the wooden garden fence. They gained height and momentum as

they flew above the greenhouse and over the vegetable patch. Rara shut her eyes tight. This was the highest she'd ever been. It also felt like the fastest speed Rara had ever travelled. The cold breeze on her face was so strong it was making her eyes water.

Bees only fly at about 15 miles an hour but to peedie Rara it felt like she was flying on a jet! Max smiled down and comforted her by brushing his soft fuzzy face across her cheek. "Look at my world Rara" he buzzed as they flew in and around the flower garden.

Rara ever so cautiously opened her eyes. She was utterly amazed and agreed it WAS a

spectacular sight. Before long she had forgotten all about how hungry and homesick she was. "This is great!" trilled Rara, admiring the fabulous views over the garden.

"Would you like to visit my house on the way back?" asked Max.

"Oh yes please Max, I'd love that" gasped Rara excitedly as she clung to him tighter than ever. They travelled towards the big tree at the edge of the garden and smoothly entered the hive. This was where Max and forty thousand members of his family lived.

The Hive

The hive was magnificent, like a huge golden palace. Rara had never seen anything so wonderful. The warm

sweet smell of honey filled her nostrils and a glow as bright as the sun shone throughout.

There were dozens of large rooms inside. Hundreds of bees were fetching and carrying honey. Beautifully sculpted pillars filled the spaces between floor and ceiling. Rivers of warm honey gushed past them. An almost inaudible buzzing sound constantly surrounded them. Rara felt safe and protected.

Max explained to Rara how the older bees taught the youngsters how to make the honey. This was an incredibly important task. These bees were called 'workers' and they were all female (funny that isn't it!) He explained how he was a 'drone', a male bee and his job along with only fourteen others was to mate with the Queen, who was the mother of every bee in the hive.

Rara was transfixed by Max's story. She couldn't believe she'd met someone with an even bigger family than hers!

It was fantastic how the huge family of bees worked together as a team to ensure

the survival of the entire hive and how the honey was their most important and special commodity.

Max and Rara entered a long golden tunnel before swiftly turning a corner into what Max described as 'the nursery.'

It was truly amazing. Hundreds of bees were placing their young into tiny beds. Alongside each baby the adult bees lay a portion of honey and then topped it off with wax to seal the baby in with its food. In the corner of the nursery were a group of bees, gently humming a lullaby, soothing the babies slowly to sleep. They swayed from side to side in time with their sweet music. It was the most beautiful scene and it made Rara feel all warm inside. She hugged Max tightly

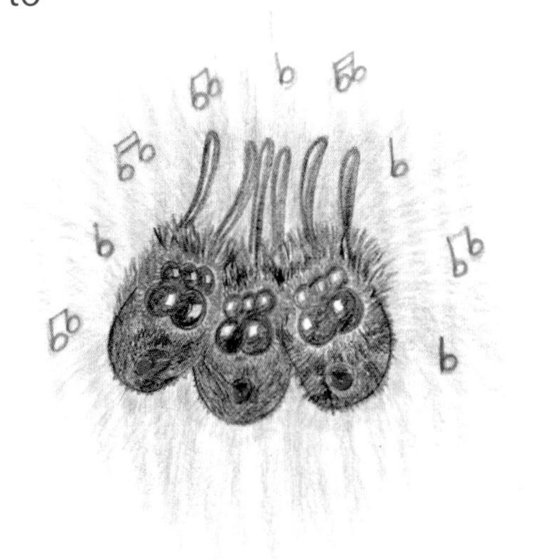

and whispered tenderly "you have the loveliest family, you are very lucky."

They both gazed around the huge nursery feeling completely happy and in Max's case, totally blessed.

As the last baby was carefully and lovingly put to bed, Max and Rara turned around and began their journey out of the hive. "Let's get you back to your family. They must be missing you by now." Max smiled and gently lifted Rara into the air once more. Rara nodded and thought how much she missed her mother and father. She wondered what they might be doing. All she wanted was to give them both a huge hug.

Up and up, higher and faster, Rara and Max flew, first out of the tree and then behind the

greenhouse and over the vegetable patch. The cool wind began to chill Rara's ears. She was completely lost in thought when "Whooah!" shouted Max as he swerved sideways. Kona and Belle had suddenly appeared bounding across the lawn, hurtling towards them. Huge slobbery canine mouths with sharp white teeth loomed ahead.

"Arrghhhhh!" shrieked Rara thinking they were about to be eaten alive by the family dogs! Max had to swiftly dart past them and fly even higher, narrowly missing the conservatory.

Rara shut her eyes and began to pray for safety. She wished to be big again and promised always to be good in future. The whole world seemed to be rapidly swirling around. Rara's eyes were nipped tightly shut for so long that she feared they'd never again reopen.

Was it real?

Rara had been so petrified that she hadn't even felt herself touch down on the grass. After a while she finally plucked up the courage to open her eyes (one at a time of course.) At once she noticed that things looked different again. The sky wasn't miles away and the grass was not huge and tall like giant trees.

Sadly Max had disappeared but everything else around her appeared to be back to normal and so was Rara!

"That was weird!" shouted Rara excitedly as she looked around the garden to make sure everything was as it should be. She patted her face and tummy and quickly checked that she was still in one piece. Wow, wait until everyone hears about this, she thought as she rushed into the house.

Rara shoved open the door and fell inside. Her parents sat wide eyed at her ungainly entrance. She clambered to her feet, then ran in and greeted them both with the biggest, tightest, squeezy hug she could muster. "I love you both so much" she said as she fell back on to the chair beside her father. A feeling of total relief crept over her entire body.

"You're awake then Sleeping Beauty" laughed father as he rubbed Rara affectionately on the head. "You had a lovely nap out there didn't you? We've been watching you for ages from the window." Rara looked at the expression on her parents faces. They were quite serious.

For once Rara's father was not joking. Had they been sitting in the conservatory just drinking tea and watching her sleep? Then had she merely dreamed of the whole shrinking experience? Was the spider and the bee saga just a figment of her imagination? Surely not, it couldn't be could it?

"B-but didn't you see me flying with the bee? It was me, in the sky" gasped Rara, arms out stretched and mouth agape.

"You'll need to wash your hands before supper Sleepy Head" said mother, "I don't know how you get so dirty. You look like you've been dragged through a hedge backwards." Mother tenderly wiped Rara's face with a hankie.

Rara walked into the downstairs bathroom feeling extremely confused. She was full of

thought as she peered into the mirror at her dirty face and slowly began to wash her hands.

Back in the conservatory Rara's brothers and sister began setting the table just the way they always did. Everyone was behaving so normally. Rara was completely bewildered.

When supper time arrived everyone sat down at the table in their usual places and mother brought in the food. "Oh, before I forget Rara" said father with a playful grin, "before she left, Wilhemia asked me to remind you to eat your food tonight, or you'll stay peedie forever!" Father's voice rose into a ghostly note as the last words left his lips. He then wiggled his fingers in a mock scary gesture. Rara groaned and rolled her eyes. Father then patted Rara softly on the arm "she also mentioned that the bee left you a gift in your pocket, whatever that means." He shrugged his shoulders and shook his head "that weird old woman gets dottier by the day!" He added a spooky laugh as he put his finger to his temple and twisted it round in a loopy motion. He then sat down, cleared his throat and began carefully inspecting his cutlery as he always did.

A cold tingly feeling began to creep over Rara's skin. She cautiously reached inside her pocket. There was something in it! She pulled it out and gazed upon it. It was a tiny green parcel.

The parcel was a partially dried up leaf wrapped around something soft and squashy. Ever so carefully Rara opened the leaf out and inside, to her absolute amazement, she found a tiny piece of golden honeycomb! In shock and disbelief Rara dropped the parcel on the dining table. It bounced across the table and stopped in front of Leo. "Sweeeeet! Is that honeycomb?" asked a forever hungry Leo.

"Yes, it most certainly looks like it" replied father lifting his specs in order to gain a better look.

Then, as quick as a flash, before anyone else could say a word, Leo popped the honeycomb into his mouth.

"Mmmmmm delicious, now what's for the main course?" He grinned and began piling food on

to his plate. Ro shook her head and mouthed the word "pig."

Everyone at the table started chatting and eating. Not one person mentioned the honeycomb or how on earth it got into Rara's pocket. Dae and Rammy began skilfully firing peas at each other across the table. Father began telling anyone who'd listen about his eventful weekend shooting. The room was abuzz with all of the usual mealtime fuss. Everyone was completely normal, everyone except Rara, she was unsure what normal was anymore.

Rara quickly consumed the entire contents of her plate and politely left the table. She didn't notice how the whole family were staring slack jawed at her empty plate.

Mother and father hugged one another and then proudly patted Rara on the head as she quietly

left the room. They had no idea what string of events had triggered Rara to eat her vegetables. They were just content that she had finally done the right thing.

Rara ventured into an empty part of the house, she needed to think . . . first of all she needed to look at the facts:

First and foremost Witchypoo was without a shadow of a doubt an extremely clever witch. One who practised magic and was fairly good at it from what Rara could tell. This thought made Rara shudder.

Secondly the worm, the giant horrible hairy spider and Max the kindly bee were very real indeed and not conjured up by Rara's sometimes overactive imagination. Double shudder!

Finally, Rara decided that her family were completely potty and wouldn't know a witch if one flew up to them on a broom stick and turned them all into wide mouthed frogs!

It would be utterly pointless trying to convince

the family about Witchypoo or Rara's peedie adventure. Forever it would have to remain one of Rara's MANY secrets!

Lessons learned

Rara decided from that moment on she would ALWAYS eat her vegetables, even the greens! Yummy! No arguments and no tantrums.

Rara also remembered to be exceedingly wary whenever old Witchypoo was around.

Most importantly, Rara vowed NEVER to wish for anything silly. Not out loud and not even quietly to herself. She had found this could be a dangerous occupation.

Rara now had a new love and deep respect for the insects in the garden. She discovered that if she was very careful and moved ever so slowly,

tired, cold bees would crawl on to her hand and warm their bodies until eventually they found the strength to fly off again. Each time she helped a bee in this way a tingly feeling warmed her tummy and she pictured the lovely bee named Max kissing her cheek. She often wondered if they'd ever meet again.

Rara also made everyone in the family promise never to disturb the bee hive hanging on the tree at the edge of the garden. Rara wanted to ensure that no harm ever came to Max or to his family.

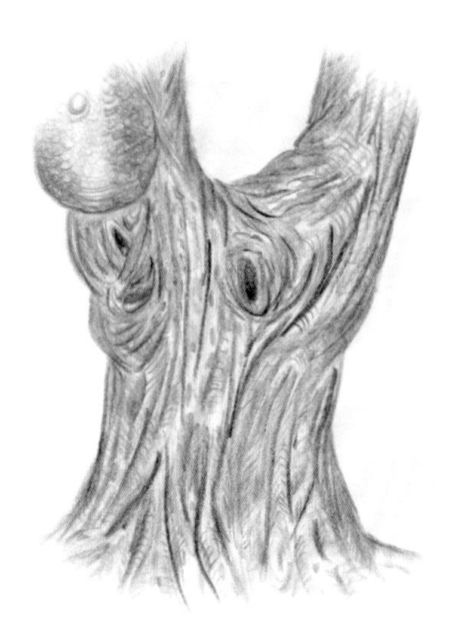

Rara remained somewhat uneasy about spiders. She understood them and admired them from afar but was eternally grateful that by eating her food, she was much bigger than them!

Whenever she remembered, Rara would un-tie the mesh on the vegetable patch and pick a few items, then place them on the ground below. Someone somewhere might need these to survive. She never forgot to tie the string back again, she didn't fancy sharing her food with every other creature in the garden!

Rara had finally discovered true happiness by simply believing in herself. She knew now that regardless of whether she was big or peedie, she was SPECIAL and could behave like a superhero. "I think I might even be able to take on some exploding goblins now!" said a triumphant young girl.

The best part about being a new and improved Rara Roggy, was that she now made her parents very, very proud. Life was perfect!